MW00977380

The Perfect Pet

by Samantha Bell

It happened just like this one day,
I never could have guessed.
I'd waited so long for a pet—
Mom finally said "yes!"

We drove down to the pet store
and I wondered what to get.
I have so many favorites;
which would make the perfect pet?

The kingdom Animalia
is where I'd start my search . . .
a bear, a slug, a killer whale,
a catfish, or a perch?

I remembered from our beach trip
the jellyfish we'd seen.
Was that the pet that I should choose?
After all, they're very clean.

But Mom said "no" to jellyfish
and worms, and insects too.
I told her, "I don't understand;
grubs don't appeal to you?"

"All invertebrates are out.
Backbones are in," she said.
"Look through phylum Chordata.
You can find one there instead."

"How about a crocodile?
It could guard our house," I said . . .
but Mom gave me a funny look
and slowly shook her head.

"No reptiles or amphibians;
they are too hard to scrub.
You just can't bathe a crocodile—
it won't fit in our tub."

"A fish," Mom said, "would be quite nice.
I think that's just the thing,
or perhaps a bird—a parakeet
or a canary that would sing."

My preference was an ostrich
or a penguin; Mom said "no."
So I decided the class Mammalia
was the way that I should go.

"How about an elephant?
A wildebeest or two . . .
a giraffe, a moose, a buffalo—
any one of them would do."

"You'd have to feed them in the yard;
they won't fit through our door.
Try the order Carnivora."
So I had to search some more.

"How 'bout a tiger, Mom?" I said.
"It could sleep with me at night.
Or perhaps a leopard or a lynx,
I don't think that they would bite."

But it's hard to take one for a walk
or keep it in the fence,
so I thought the family Canidae
would make a lot more sense.

"I know! I know!" I said to Mom.
"I know just the pet we need.
It's fierce but loyal, and smart too—
a wolf with lightning speed."

"Or how about an arctic fox—
white in winter, gray in spring?
Or a coyote, genus *Canis*—
I hear they eat most anything."

"Not quite," Mom said, "but you're close
to a pet I had in mind.
Keep looking for a Canidae
and see what you can find."

Then *Canis lupus familiaris*
gently licked me on the hand.
This furry species liked me
and it seemed to understand.

"What a friendly pup!" I said,
as he chewed upon my thumb.
I thought of how much fun it'd be
to teach him "sit" and "come."

I could take him walking in the park
or play fetch with him outside.
I could bring him in the car with me
and take him for a ride.

"You know," Mom said, "if he comes home,
you must care for him each day.
You must give him food and water
and take him out to run and play."

"You'll brush the tangles from his fur
and give him a weekly bath.
You'll fill in every hole he digs . . ."
I began to do the math.

"... You must keep him from the garbage
and not let him eat your toys.
And if the baby's sleeping late,
he can't make any noise."

"If he makes a mess inside the house,
you'll have to clean it up."
Then I really wasn't sure
if my pet should be this pup.

Pet Store

I rubbed his head, then put him back.
I knew we couldn't stay—
'cause my new pet just wasn't here . . .
but from the kingdom Plantae.

For Creative Minds

Animal Classification

If you have ever sorted candy or toys into piles, you are grouping them by some characteristic. You might sort candy by the shape or by what's in the candy. Or you might sort some types of candy by color. You can sort toys by how you use them, where you use them, or by size. When you sort things, you are classifying them by some characteristic.

Scientists sort things too. They sort all living things into groups to help us understand and connect how things relate to each other. This sorting of living things is called **taxonomy**. Scientists ask questions to help them sort or classify animals.

- Does it have a skeleton? If so, is the skeleton inside (endoskeleton) or outside (exoskeleton) of the body?
- Does it get oxygen from the air through lungs or from the water through gills?
- Does it have a backbone?
- What type of skin covering does it have?
- Does the animal have a steady body temperature (warm-blooded) or does it use the heat of the sun or surrounding water to warm itself (cold-blooded)?
- Are the babies born alive or do they hatch from eggs?
- Does the baby drink milk from its mother?

The first and broadest sort is a kingdom. All living things can be sorted into one of the five commonly-accepted kingdoms (Monera, Protista, Fungi, Plantae, and Animalia).

Next, living things are sorted into phyla. In the animal kingdom, a scientist asks if the animal has (or ever had) a backbone. If the answer is "no," the animal is an invertebrate. If the answer is "yes," the animal is a vertebrate. All animals with backbones are in the phylum Chordata, in a subphylum called Vertebrata. Scientists continue to ask questions and sort into more specific categories.

Once identified, living things are named by their genus and species.

Kingdom: Animalia

Phylum: Chordata

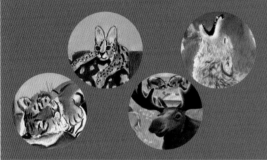 

Class: Mammalia

   Order: Carnivora

 Family: Canidae

 Genus: *Canis*

Species: *lupus*
Subspecies: *familiaris*

 Canis lupus familiaris: the domestic dog

There are five major classes of vertebrates:

Fish:
- most have scales covered with a thin layer of slime
- backbone (vertebrate)
- inside skeleton (endoskeleton)
- gills to breathe
- babies are either born alive or hatch from eggs
- cold-blooded

Amphibians:
- soft, moist skin
- backbone (vertebrate)
- inside skeleton (endoskeleton)
- most hatchlings are called larvae or tadpoles and live in water, using gills to breathe
- as they grow, they develop legs and lungs and move onto land
- cold-blooded

Reptiles:
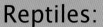
- dry scales or plates
- backbone (vertebrate)
- inside skeleton (endoskeleton); most turtles also have a hard outer shell
- lungs to breathe
- most hatch from leathery eggs
- cold-blooded

Birds:
- feathers
- backbone (vertebrate)
- inside skeleton (endoskeleton)
- lungs to breathe
- hatch from eggs
- warm-blooded

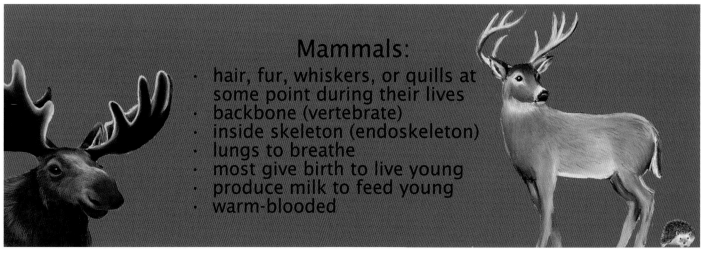

Mammals:
- hair, fur, whiskers, or quills at some point during their lives
- backbone (vertebrate)
- inside skeleton (endoskeleton)
- lungs to breathe
- most give birth to live young
- produce milk to feed young
- warm-blooded

Compare and Contrast the Animals

Which animals have fur and which have feathers or scales?
Which do *you* think would make a good pet? Why?

Answers: Fur: dog and rabbits. Feathers: penguin and cockatiel parrots. Scales: corn snake, beta fish, and chameleon.

To my mom, Karole Schweizer, who helped all of us find our perfect pets.

Thanks to Hattie Frederick, former interpretive ranger at Acadia National Park and National Association for Interpretation Certified Interpretive Guide, for verifying the accuracy of the information in this book.

Library of Congress Cataloging-in-Publication Data

Bell, Samantha, author, illustrator.
  The perfect pet / by Samantha Bell.
    pages cm
  Summary: Starting with the Kingdom Animalia, the child walks through the various animal classes trying to choose the perfect pet.
  ISBN 978-1-60718-621-2 (english hardcover) -- ISBN 978-1-60718-633-5 (english pbk.) -- ISBN 978-1-60718-645-8 (english ebook (downloadable)) -- ISBN 978-1-60718-669-4 (interactive english/spanish ebook (web-based)) -- ISBN 978-1-60718-718-9 (spanish hardcover) -- ISBN 978-1-60718-657-1 (spanish ebook (downloadable)) [1. Stories in rhyme. 2. Pets--Fiction. 3. Animals--Classification--Fiction.] I. Bell, Samantha. Mascota perfecta. II. Title.
  PZ8.3.B413Pe 2013
  [E]--dc23
                                        2012045098

The Perfect Pet: Original Title in English
La mascota perfecta: Spanish Title
Translated into Spanish by Rosalyna Toth

Lexile® Level: 590L Lexile® Code: AD
Curriculum keywords: animal classification, compare/contrast, rhythm or rhyme

Manufactured in China, June, 2013
This product conforms to CPSIA 2008
First Printing

Sylvan Dell Publishing
Mt. Pleasant, SC 29464
www.SylvanDellPublishing.com